The "Ahh..." Goodnight Book
By Julie Hanney

Laugh, relax and snuggle your way to dreamland

Special thanks to:
Kyle, Ryan and Amy for teaching me about energetic kids :-)
My husband Derwyn for being so awesome
My Mom and Dad for reading to me

Copyright 2020 Julie Hanney
All text by Julie Hanney
All photos used by generous permission by:
www.pexels.com
pixabay.com
www.publicdomainpictures.net

ISBN 9781655201646

Let's get ready to snuggle!

Good evening. I know it's getting late but…
Are you ready for a challenge?

Okay, here we go:
Don't look up.

And don't look...

**d
o
w
n.**

Don't look

to the **side.**

And by all means,
<u>please</u>

don't roll your head around.

Don't wiggle your little fingers.

Keep them verrrrry still.

Okay, wiggle just one finger.

You choose which one.

(Now, this one will be hard.)
Are you ready?

Try not to think about **yesterday.**

Thinking...

not thinking...

clearing the mind...

You thought about yesterday, didn't you?

(That's okay. This guy did too.)

Since we are talking about yesterday… can you name one thing you are grateful for that happened yesterday?

Ready, set, go…

How about today? What is something good that happened today?

For this next challenge try super, duper, **flooper** hard:

Don't think about tomorrow.

(It's hard, huh?)

Are you **still** not thinking about tomorrow?

(I'm trying!)

Whew, we did it!!!
(High five!)

Now let's go ahead and think about tomorrow.

What is something you are looking forward to tomorrow?

(I hope it's something awesome.)

New challenge alert!!!

Are you ready

?

This is a little game
we like to call
"feet freeze."

It's a simple game, really.

The object is:

Don't move your feet!

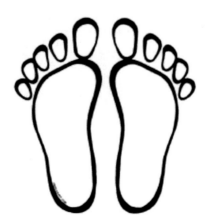

Just **feel** your feet without moving them.

So still,
so still,
so incredibly still.

Nice! Now wiggle your feet and bend your toes and roll your ankles! Your feet are having…

A PARTY!

(Woo hoo! Foot party! My favorite kind of party!)

And... **stop!**
Be very still. Good, good.

Keep being verrrrrry still.
Even more still.

Shhh...
Still.
Yes.

(I'm truly impressed!)

Next question: Can you feel yourself breathing?

Put your hand on your tummy and take a deep breath in…

and hold it...

Then let it out with a big
"ahh…"

That feels good, doesn't it?

And now it's <u>really</u> time for sleep,
my little friend.

I know, I know...

Today was
fun and
reading is
fun and
laughing is
seriously so
much fun...

But humans need to sleep.
Animals need to sleep too.
When we sleep, our brains and bodies
get charged up so we have energy
for the next day.

And believe it or not, you *grow*
at night when you are sleeping!

Let's get you into a
snuggly position
with the blankets just
how you like them.

And I will give you a
snuggle, snuggle, snuggle.

And here we go: close one eye.

(Like this li'l guy.)

Nicely done.

Open your eye again.

And now let's
close the other eye.

This is awesome.
You are almost ready.

Okay, this is it:

Close *both* eyes.

Okay, first look at this adorable puppy,
then close both eyes.

Now I will say a blessing:

"May this child have
good dreams,
a good rest
and a good grow."

One more gentle breath in…

and let it out with a sigh,
"Ahh…"

Good night, dear one,

good night.

Sleep tight.

Twinkle, twinkle little star

How I wonder what you are

Up above the world so high

Like a diamond in the sky

Twinkle, twinkle little star

How I wonder what you are

Sparkle, sparkle glowing moon

How you make me sing a tune

In the sky you cast a glow

On your friends so far below

Sparkle, sparkle glowing moon

How you make me sing a tune

About the author

Julie Hanney is a mom, author, teacher, pianist, composer and a lover of nature. Her three children are grown now, but when they were small a book like this would have saved the day… umm, night. ;-)

Progressive relaxation and deep breathing are wonderful techniques for children and adults to use to help calm down before bed or whenever the need arises. Expressing gratitude has been shown to improve psychological and physical health, enhance empathy, reduce aggression, improve sleep and build self-esteem.

Julie has been committed to children's education for many years and has worked with children as a piano teacher, classroom music teacher, choir director, licensed Kindermusik instructor, ukulele teacher, Sunday School teacher and more.

Another book by Julie Hanney is: "Looks Easy, Sounds Hard" – Inventive piano solos for beginners of all ages who want to make real music. This is a truly unique songbook with 15 original pieces in a variety of styles. These songs are a gift for people young and old who want to play music that is moving, inventive, beautiful, jazzy and fun. And they truly do sound "harder" than they look! It is available on Amazon.com. More info can also be found at www.juliehanneypiano.com.

In addition to writing books, Julie has recorded two solo piano albums as of this printing. They are titled *Painting in Sound* and *A Peace-Filled Christmas*. Both are available on various streaming platforms like Spotify and Apple Music. Physical and digital CDs can be purchased on cdbaby.com and iTunes. More info about Julie's solo piano projects and samples are on her website: www.juliehanneypiano.com.

Julie is deeply grateful to these contributors of free images for this book:
www.pexels.com
pixabay.com
www.publicdomainpictures.net

Happy reading. Happy snuggling. Happy sleeping.

Julie Hanney

Made in the USA
Columbia, SC
26 December 2020